The Rector of Veilbye

Steen Blicher

The Rector of Veilbye by Steen Steensen Blicher. First published in 1829. This edition Copyright © 2014 Enhanced Media. All rights reserved.

ISBN-10: 1500384755
ISBN-13: 978-1500384753

These extracts from the diary of Erik Sorensen, District Judge, followed by two written statements by the rector of Also, give a complete picture of the terrible events that took place in the parish of Veilbye during Judge Sorensen's first year of office. Should anyone be inclined to doubt the authenticity of these documents let him at least have no doubt about the story, which is, alas! only too sadly true. The memory of these events is still fresh in the district, and the events themselves have been the direct cause of a change in the method of criminal trials. A suspected murderer is now tried through all the courts before his conviction can be determined. Readers versed in the history of law will doubtless know by this during what epoch the story is laid.

CONTENTS

PART ONE   Page 5

PART TWO   Page 20

Who was Steen Blicher? An Appreciation.   Page 24

PART ONE

From the Diary of District Judge Erik Sorensen

Now am I, unworthy one, by the grace of God made judge over this district. May the Great Judge above give me wisdom and uprightness that I may fulfill my difficult task in all humility! From the Lord alone cometh judgment.

It is not good that man should live alone. Now that I am able to support a wife I will look about me for a helpmeet. I hear much good said about the daughter of the Rector of Veilbye. Since her mother's death she has been a wise and economical keeper of her father's house. And as she and her brother the student are the only children, she will inherit a tidy sum when the old man dies.

Morten Bruus of Ingvorstrup was here to-day and wanted to make me a present of a fat calf. But I answered him in the words of Moses, "Cursed be he who taketh gifts." He is of a very quarrelsome nature, a sharp bargainer, and a boastful talker. I do not want to have any dealings with him, except through my office as judge.

I have prayed to God for wisdom and I have consulted with my own heart, and I believe that Mistress Mette Quist is the only woman with whom I could live and die. But I will watch her for a time in secret. Beauty is deceptive and charm is a dangerous thing. But I must say that she is the most beautiful woman I have yet seen.

I think that Morten Bruus a very disagreeable person—I scarcely know why myself. But whenever I see him something comes over me, something that is like the memory of an evil dream. And yet it is so vague and so faint, that I could not say whether I had really ever seen the man in my dreams or not. It may be a sort of presentiment of evil; who knows?

He was here again and offered me a pair of horses—beautiful animals—at a ridiculously low price. It looked queer to me. I know that he paid seventy thalers for them, and he wanted to let me have them for the same price. They are at the least worth one hundred thalers, if not more. Was it intended for a bribe? He may have another lawsuit pending. I do not want his horses.

I paid a visit to the Rector of Veilbye to-day. He is a fine, God- fearing man, but somewhat quick-tempered and dictatorial. And he is close with his money, too, as I could see. Just as I arrived a peasant was with him trying to be let off the payment of part of his tithe. The man is surely a rogue, for the sum is not large. But the rector talked to him as I wouldn't have talked to a dog, and the more, he talked the more violent he became.

Well, we all have our faults. The rector meant well in spite of his violence, for later on he told his daughter to give the man a sandwich and a good glass of beer. She is certainly a charming and sensible girl. She greeted me in a modest and friendly manner, and my heart beat so that I could scarcely say a word in reply. My head farm hand served in the rectory three years. I will question him —— one often hears a straight and true statement from servants.

A surprise! My farm hand Rasmus tells me that Morten Bruus came a-wooing to the rectory at Veilbye some years back, but was sent away with a refusal. The rector seemed to be pleased with him, for the man is rich. But his daughter would not hear to it at all. Pastor Soren may have tried hard to persuade her to consent at first. But when he saw how much she disliked the man he let her do as she would. It was not pride on her part, Rasmus said, for she is as simple and modest as she is good and beautiful. And she knows that her own father is peasant-born as well as Bruus.

Now I know what the Ingvorstrup horses were intended for. They were to blind the judge and to lead him aside from the narrow path of righteousness. The rich Morten Bruns covets poor Ole Anderson's peat moor and pasture land. It would have been a good bargain for Morten even at seventy thalers. But no indeed, my good fellow, you don't know Erik Sorensen!

Rector Soren Quist of Veilbye came to see me this morning. He has a new coachman, Niels Bruus, brother to the owner of Ingvorstrup. Neils is lazy and impertinent. The rector wanted him arrested, but he had no witnesses to back up his complaint. I advised him to get rid of the man somehow, or else to get along with him the best he could until the latter's time was up. The rector was somewhat hasty at first, but later on he listened calmly and thanked me for my good advice. He is inclined to be violent at times, but can always be brought to listen to reason. We parted good friends.

I spent a charming day in Veilbye yesterday. The rector was not at home, but Mistress Mette received me with great friendliness. She sat by the door spinning when I arrived, and it seemed to me that she blushed. It was hardly polite for me to wait so long before speaking. When I sit in judgment I never lack for words, but in the presence of this innocent maiden I am as stupid as the veriest simpleton of a chicken thief. But I finally found my voice and the time passed quickly until the rector's return. Then Mistress Mette left us and did not return until she brought in our supper.

Just as she stepped through the doorway the rector was saying to me, "Isn't it about time that you should think of entering into the holy estate of matrimony?" (We had just been speaking of a recent very fine wedding in the neighborhood.) Mistress Mette heard the words and flushed a deep red. Her father laughed and said to her, "I can see, my dear daughter, that you have been standing before the fire."

I shall take the good man's advice and will very soon try my fate with her. For I think I may take the rector's words to be a secret hint that he would not object to me as a son-in-law. And the daughter? Was her blush a favorable sign?

Poor Ole Anderson keeps his peat moor and his pasture land, but rich Morten Bruus is angry at me because of it. When he heard the decision he closed his eyes and set his lips tight, and his face was as pale as a whitewashed wall. But he controlled himself and as he went out he called back to his adversary, "Wish you joy of the bargain, Ole Anderson. The peat bog won't beggar me, and the cattle at Ingvorstrup have all the hay they can eat." I could hear his loud laughter outside and the cracking of his whip. It is not easy to have to sit in judgment. Every decision makes but one enemy the more.

Yesterday was the happiest day of my life. We celebrated our betrothal in the Rectory of Veilbye. My future father-in-law spoke to the text, "I gave my handmaid into thy bosom" (Genesis xvi, 5). His words touched my heart. I had not believed that this serious and sometimes brusque man could talk so sweetly. When the solemnity was over, I received the first kiss from my sweet betrothed, and the assurance of her great love for me.

At supper and later on we were very merry. Many of the dead mother's kin were present. The rector's family were too far away. After supper we danced until daybreak and there was no expense spared in the food and wine. My future father-in-law was the strongest man present, and could easily drink all the others under the table. The wedding is to take place in six weeks. God grant us rich blessings.

It is not good that my future father-in-law should have this Niels Bruus in his service. He is a defiant fellow, a worthy brother of him of Ingvorstrup. If it were I, he should have his wages and be turned off, the sooner the better. But the good rector is stubborn and insists that Niels shall serve out his time. The other day he gave the fellow a box on the ear, at which Niels cried out that he would make him pay for it. The rector told me of this himself, for no one else had been present. I talked to Niels, but he would scarcely answer me. I fear he has a stubborn and evil nature. My sweet betrothed also en-treats her father to send the fellow away, but the rector will not listen to reason. I do not know what the old man will do when his daughter leaves his home for mine. She saves him much worry and knows how to make all things smooth and easy. She will be a sweet wife for me.

As I thought, it turned out badly. But there is one good thing about it,

Niels has now run off of himself. The rector is greatly angered, but I rejoice in secret that he is rid of that dangerous man. Bruus will probably seek retaliation, but we have law and justice in the land to order such matters.

This was the way of it: The rector had ordered Niels to dig up a bit of soil in the garden. After a time when he went out himself to look at the work, he found Niels leaning on his spade eating nuts. He had not even begun to dig. The rector scolded him, but the fellow answered that he had not taken service as a gardener. He received a good box on the ear for that. At this he threw away his spade and swore valiantly at his master. The old rector lost his temper entirely, seized the spade and struck at the man several times. He should not have done this, for a spade is a dangerous weapon, especially in the hands of a man as strong as is the pastor in spite of his years. Niels fell to the ground as if dead. But when the pastor bent over him in alarm, he sprang up suddenly, jumped the hedge and ran away to the woods.

This is the story of the unfortunate affair as my father-in-law tells it to me. My beloved Mette is much worried about it. She fears the man may do harm to the cattle, or set fire to the house, or in some such way take his revenge. But I tell her there is little fear of that.

Three weeks more and my beloved leaves her father's house for mine. She has been here and has gone over the house and the farm. She is much pleased with everything and praises our orderliness. She is an angel, and all who know her say that I am indeed a fortunate man. To God be the praise!

Strange, where that fellow Niels went to! Could he have left the country altogether? It is an unpleasant affair in any case, and there are murmurings and secret gossip among the peasants. The talk has doubtless started in Ingvorstrup. It would not be well to have the rector hear it. He had better have taken my advice, but it is not my province to school a servant of God, and a man so much older than I. The idle gossip may blow over ere long. I will go to Veilbye to-morrow and find out if he has heard anything.

The bracelet the goldsmith has made for me is very beautiful. I am sure it will please my sweet Mette.

My honored father-in-law is much distressed and downhearted. Malicious tongues have repeated to him the stupid gossip that is going about in the district. Morten Bruus is reported to have said that "he would force the rector to bring back his brother, if he had to dig him out of the earth." The fellow may be in hiding somewhere, possibly at Ingvorstrup. He has certainly disappeared completely, and no one seems to know where he is. My poor betrothed is much grieved and worried. She is alarmed by bad dreams and by presentiments of evil to come.

God have mercy on us all! I am so overcome by shock and horror that

I can scarcely hold the pen. It has all come in one terrible moment, like a clap of thunder. I take no account of time, night and morning are the same to me and the day is but a sudden flash of lightning destroying the proud castle of my hopes and desires. A venerable man of God—the father of my betrothed—is in prison! And as a suspected murderer! There is still hope that he may be innocent. But this hope is but as a straw to a drowning man. A terrible suspicion rests upon him—And I, unhappy man that I am, must be his judge. And his daughter is my betrothed bride! May the Saviour have pity on us!

It was yesterday that this horrible thing came. About half an hour before sunrise Morten Bruus came to my house and had with him the cotter Jens Larsen of Veilbye, and the widow and daughter of the shepherd of that parish. Morten Bruus said to me that he had the Rector of Veilbye under suspicion of having killed his brother Niels. I answered that I had heard some such talk but had regarded it as idle and malicious gossip, for the rector himself had assured me that the fellow had run away. "If that was so," said Morten, "if Niels had really intended to run away, he would surely at first come to me to tell me of it. But it is not so, as these good people can prove to you, and I demand that you shall hear them as an officer of the law."

"Think well of what you are doing," I said. "Think it over well, Morten Bruus, and you, my good people. You are bringing a terrible accusation against a respected and unspotted priest and man of God. If you can prove nothing, as I strongly suspect, your accusations may cost you dear."

"Priest or no priest," cried Bruus, "it is written, 'thou shalt not kill!' And also is it written, that the authorities bear the sword of justice for all men. We have law and order in the land, and the murderer shall not escape his punishment, even if he have the district judge for a son-in-law."

I pretended not to notice his thrust and began, "It shall be as you say. Kirsten Mads' daughter, what is it that you know of this matter in which Morten Bruus accuses your rector? Tell the truth, and the truth only, as you would tell it before the judgment seat of the Almighty. The law will demand from you that you shall later repeat your testimony under oath."

The woman told the following story: The day on which Niels Bruus was said to have run away from the rectory, she and her daughter were passing along the road near the rectory garden a little after the noon hour. She heard some one calling and saw that it was Niels Bruus looking out through the garden hedge. He asked the daughter if she did not want some nuts and told the women that the rector had ordered him to dig in the garden, but that he did not take the command very seriously and would much rather eat nuts. At that moment they heard a door open in the house and Niels said, "Now I'm in for a scolding." He dropped back behind the hedge and the women heard a quarrel in the garden. They could hear the words distinctly but they could see nothing, as the hedge was too high. They heard the rector cry, "I'll punish you, you dog. I'll strike you dead at my feet!" Then they heard several sounding slaps, and they heard Niels curse back at the rector and call him evil names. The rector did not answer this, but the women heard two dull blows and saw the head of a spade and part of the handle rise and fall twice over the hedge. Then it was very quiet in the garden, and the widow and her daughter were frightened and hurried on to their cattle in the field. The daughter gave the same testimony, word for word. I asked them if they had not seen Niels Bruus coming out of the garden. But they said they had not, although they had turned back several times to look.

This accorded perfectly with what the rector had told me. It was not strange that the women had not seen the man run out of the garden, for he had gone toward the wood which is on the opposite side of the garden from the highroad. I told Marten Bruus that this testimony was no proof of the supposed murder, especially as the rector himself had narrated the entire occurrence to me exactly as the women had described it. But he smiled bitterly and asked me to examine the third witness, which I proceeded to do.

Jens Larsen testified that he was returning late one evening from Tolstrup (as he remembered, it was not the evening of Niels Bruus's disappearance, but the evening of the following day), and was passing the rectory garden on the easterly side by the usual footpath. From the garden he heard a noise as of some one digging in the earth. He was frightened at first for it was very late, but the moon shone brightly and he thought he would see who it was that was at work in the garden at that hour. He put off his wooden shoes and pushed aside the twigs of the hedge until he had made a peep hole. In the garden he saw the rector in his usual house coat, a white woolen nightcap on his head. He was busily smoothing down the earth with the flat of his spade. There was nothing else to be seen. Just then the rector had started and partly turned toward the hedge, and the witness, fearing he might be discovered, slipped down and ran home hastily.

Although I was rather surprised that the rector should be working in his garden at so late an hour, I still saw nothing in this statement that could arouse suspicion of murder. I gave the complainant a solemn warning and advised him not only to let fall his accusation, but to put an end to the talk in the parish. He replied, "Not until I see what it is that the rector buried in his garden."

"That will be too late," I said. "You are playing a dangerous game. Dangerous to your own honor and welfare."

"I owe it to my brother," he replied, "and I demand that the authorities shall not refuse me assistance."

My office compelled me to accede to his demands. Accompanied by the accuser and his witnesses I took my way to Veilbye. My heart was very heavy, not so much because of any fear that we might find the missing man buried in the garden, but because of the surprise and distress I must cause the rector and my beloved. As we went on our way I thought over how severely the law would allow me to punish the calumniators. But alas, Merciful Heavens! What a terrible discovery was in store for me!

I had wished to have a moment alone with the rector to prepare him for what was coming. But as I drove through the gate Morten Bruus spurred his horse past me and galloped up to the very door of the house just as the rector opened it. Bruus cried out in his very face, "People say that you have killed my brother and buried him in your garden. I am come with the district judge to seek for him."

The poor rector was so shocked and astounded that he could not find a word to answer. I sprang from my wagon and addressed him: "You have now heard the accusation. I am forced by my office to fulfill this man's demands. But your own honor demands that the truth shall be known and the mouth of slander silenced."

"It is hard enough," began the rector finally, "for a man in my position to have to clear himself from such a suspicion. But come with me. My garden and my entire house are open to you."

We went through the house to the garden. On the way we met my betrothed, who was startled at seeing Bruus. I managed to whisper hastily to her, "Do not be alarmed, dear heart. Your enemies are going to their own destruction." Marten Bruus led the way to the eastern side of the garden near the hedge. We others followed with the rector's farm hands, whom he himself had ordered to join us with spades.

The accuser stood and looked about him until we approached. Then he pointed to one spot. "This looks as if the earth had been disturbed lately. Let us begin here."

"Go to work at once," commanded the rector angrily.

The men set to work, but they were not eager enough to suit Bruus, who seized a spade himself to fire them on. A few strokes only sufficed to show that the firm earth of this particular spot had not been touched for many years. We all rejoiced—except Bruus— and the rector was very happy. He triumphed openly over his accuser, and laughed at him, "Can't you find anything, you libeler?"

Bruus did not answer. He pondered for a few moments, then called out, "Jens Larsen, where was it you saw the rector digging?"

Jens Larsen had been standing to one side with his hands folded, watching the work. At Bruus's words he aroused himself as if from a dream, looked about him and pointed to a corner of the garden several yards from where we stood. "I think it was over there."

"What's that, Jens!" cried the rector angrily. "When did I dig here?"

Paying no heed to this, Morten Bruus called the men to the corner in question. The earth here was covered by some withered cabbage stalks, broken twigs, and other brush which he pushed aside hurriedly. The work began anew.

I stood by the rector talking calmly with him about the punishment we could mete out to the dastardly accuser, when one of the men suddenly cried out with an oath. We looked toward them; there lay a hat half buried in the loose earth. "We have found him," cried Bruus. "That is Niels's hat; I would know it anywhere."

My blood seemed turned to ice. All my hopes dashed to the ground. "Dig! Dig!" cried the bloodthirsty accuser, working himself with all his might. I looked at the rector. He was ghastly pale, staring with wide-open eyes at the horrible spot.

Another shout! A hand was stretched up through the earth as if to greet the workers. "See there!" screamed Bruus. "He is holding out his hand to me. Wait a little, Brother Niels! You will soon be avenged!"

The entire corpse was soon uncovered. It was the missing man. His face was not recognizable, as decomposition had begun, and the nose was broken and laid flat by a blow. But all the garments, even to the shirt with his name woven into it, were known to those who stood there. In one ear was a leaden ring, which, as we all knew, Niels Bruus had worn for many years.

"Now, priest," cried Marten Bruus, "come and lay your hand on this dead man if you dare to!"

"Almighty God!" sighed the rector, looking up to heaven, "Thou art my witness that I am innocent. I struck him, that I confess, and I am bitterly sorry for it. But he ran away. God Almighty alone knows who buried him here."

"Jens Larsen knows also," cried Bruus, "and I may find more witnesses. Judge! You will come with me to examine his servants. But first of all I demand that you shall arrest this wolf in sheep's clothing."

Merciful God, how could I doubt any longer? The truth was clear to all of us. But I was ready to sink into the earth in my shock and horror. I was about to say to the rector that he must prepare to follow me, when he himself spoke to me, pale and trembling like an aspen leaf. "Appearances are against me," he said, but this is the work of the devil and his angels. There is One above who will bring my innocence to light. Come, judge, I will await my fate in fetters. Comfort my daughter. Remember that she is your betrothed bride."

He had scarcely uttered the words when I heard a scream and a fall behind us. It was my beloved who lay unconscious on the ground. I thought at first that she was dead, and God knows I wished that I could lie there dead beside her. I raised her in my arms, but her father took her from me and carried her into the house. I was called to examine the wound on the dead man's head. The cut was not deep, but it had evidently fractured the skull, and had plainly been made by a blow from a spade or some similar blunt instrument.

Then we all entered the house. My beloved had revived again. She fell on my neck and implored me, in the name of God, to help her father in his terrible need. She begged me by the memory of our mutual love to let her follow him to prison, to which I consented. I myself accompanied him to Grenaa, but with a mournful heart. None of us spoke a word on the sad journey. I parted from them in deep distress. The corpse was laid in a coffin and will be buried decently to-morrow in Veilbye churchyard.

To-morrow I must give a formal hearing to the witnesses. God be merciful to me, unfortunate man!

Would that I had never obtained this position for which I—fool that I am—strove so hard.

As the venerable man of God was brought before me, fettered hand and foot, I felt as Pilate must have felt as they brought Christ before him. It was to me as if my beloved—God grant her comfort, she lies ill in Grenaa—had whispered to me, "Do nothing against that good man!"

Oh, if he only were innocent, but I see no hope!

The three first witnesses repeated their testimony under oath, word for word. Then came statements by the rector's two farm hands and the dairy maid. The men had been in the kitchen on the fatal day, and as the windows were open they had heard the quarrel between the rector and Niels. As the widow had stated, these men had also heard the rector say, "I will strike you dead at my feet!" They further testified that the rector was very quick-tempered, and that when angered he did not hesitate to strike out with whatever came into his hand. He had struck a former hand once with a heavy maul.

The girl testified that on the night Jens Larsen claimed to have seen the rector in the garden, she had lain awake and heard the creaking of the garden door. When she looked out of the window she had seen the rector in his dressing gown and nightcap go into the garden. She could not see what he was doing there. But she heard the door creak again about an hour later.

When the witnesses had been heard, I asked the unfortunate man whether he would make a confession, or else, if he had anything to say in his own defense. He crossed his hands over his breast and said, "So help me God, I will tell the truth. I have nothing more to say than what I have said already. I struck the dead man with my spade. He fell down, but jumped up in a moment and ran away from the garden out into the woods.

What may have happened to him there, or how he came to be buried in my garden, this I do not know. When Jens Larsen and my servant testify that they saw me at night in the garden, either they are lying, or Satan has blinded them. I can see this—unhappy man that I am—that I have no one to turn to for help here on earth. Will He who is in heaven be silent also, then must I bow to His inscrutable will." He bowed his head with a deep sigh.

Some of those present began to weep, and a murmur arose that he might possibly be innocent. But this was only the effect of the momentary sympathy called out by his attitude. My own heart indeed spoke for him. But the judge's heart may not dare to dictate to his brain or to his conscience. My conviction forced me to declare that the rector had killed Niels Bruus, but certainly without any premeditation or intention to do so. It is true that Niels Bruus had often been heard to declare that he would "get even with the rector when the latter least expected it." But it is not known that he had fulfilled his threat in any way. Every man clings to life and honor as long as he can. Therefore the rector persists in his denial. My poor, dear Mette! She is lost to me for this life at least, just as I had learned to love her so dearly.

I have had a hard fight to fight to-day. As I sat alone, pondering over this terrible affair in which it is my sad lot to have to give judgment, the door opened and the rector's daughter—I may no longer call her my betrothed—rushed in and threw herself at my feet. I raised her up, clasped her in my arms and we wept together in silence. I was first to control myself. "I know what you would say, dear heart. You want me to save your father. Alas, God help us poor mortals, I cannot do it! Tell me, dearest one, tell me truly, do you yourself believe your father to be innocent?"

She crossed her hands on her heart and sobbed, "I do not know!" Then she burst into tears again. "But he did not bury him in the garden," she continued after a few moments. "The man may have died in the wood from the blow. That may have happened—"

"But, dearest heart," I said, "Jens Larsen and the girl saw your father in the garden that night."

She shook her head slowly and answered, "The evil one blinded their eyes." She wept bitterly again.

"Tell me, beloved," she began again, after a while, "tell me frankly this much. If God sends us no further enlightenment in this unfortunate affair, what sentence must you give?"

She gazed anxiously at me, her lips trembling.

"If I did not believe," I began slowly, "that anyone else in my place would be more severe than I, then I would gladly give up my position at once and refuse to speak the verdict. But I dare not conceal from you that the mildest sentence that God, our king, and our laws demand is, a life for a life."

She sank to her knees, then sprang up again, fell back several steps as if afraid of me, and cried out: "Would you murder my father? Would you murder your betrothed bride? See here! See this!" She came nearer and held up her hand with my ring on it before my eyes. "Do you see this betrothal ring? What was it my father said when you put this ring upon my finger? 'I have given my maid unto thy bosom!' But you, you thrust the steel deep into my bosom!"

Alas, every one of her words cut deep into my own heart. "Dearest love," I cried, "do not speak so. You thrust burning irons into my heart. What would you have me do? Acquit him, when the laws of God and man condemn?"

She was silent, sobbing desperately.

"One thing I can do," I continued. "If it be wrong may God forgive me. If the trial goes on to an end his life is forfeited, there is no hope except in flight. If you can arrange an escape I will close my eyes. I will not see or hear anything. As soon as your father was imprisoned, I wrote to your brother in Copenhagen. He can arrive any moment now. Talk to him, make friends with the jailer. If you lack money, all I have is yours."

When I had finished her face flushed with joy, and she threw her arms about my neck. "God bless you for these words. Were my brother but here, he will know what to do. But where shall we go?" her tone changed suddenly and her arms dropped. "Even should we find a refuge in a foreign country I could never see you again!" Her tone was so sad that my heart was near to breaking.

"Beloved," I exclaimed, "I will find you wherever you may hide yourself! Should our money not be sufficient to support us I can work for us all. I have learned to use the ax and the hoe."

She rejoiced again and kissed me many times. We prayed to God to bless our undertaking and parted with glad hearts. I also hoped for the best. Doubts assail me, but God will find for us some light in this darkness.

Two more new witnesses. They bring nothing good, I fear, for Bruus announced them with an expression I did not like. He has a heart of stone, which can feel nothing but malice and bitterness. I give them a hearing tomorrow. I feel as if they had come to bear witness against me myself. May God strengthen my heart.

All is over. He has confessed.

The court was in session and the prisoner had been brought in to hear the testimony of the new witnesses. These men stated as follows: On the night in question they were walking along the path that led between the woods and the rectory garden. A man with a large sack on his back came out of the woods and walked ahead of them toward the garden. They could not see his face, but in the bright moonlight his figure was clearly visible, and they could see that he wore a loose green garment, like a dressing gown, and a white nightcap. The man disappeared through an opening in the rectory garden fence.

Scarcely had the first witness ended his statement when the rector turned ghastly pale, and gasped, in a voice that could scarcely be heard, "I am ill." They gave him a chair.

Bruus turned to his neighbor and exclaimed audibly, "That helped the rector's memory."

The prisoner did not hear the words, but motioned to me and said, "Lead me back to my prison. I will talk to you there." They did as he demanded.

We set out at once for Grenaa. The rector was in the wagon with the jailer and the gendarme, and I rode beside them.

When the door of the cell was opened my beloved was making up her father's bed, and over a chair by the bedside hung the fatal green dressing gown. My dear betrothed greeted me with a cry of joy, as she believed that I was come to set her father free. She hung about the old man's neck, kissing away the tears that rolled unhindered down his cheeks. I had not the heart to undeceive her, and I sent her out into the town to buy some things for us.

"Sit down, dear friend," said the rector, when we were alone. He seated himself on the bed, staring at the ground with eyes that did not see. Finally he turned toward me where I sat trembling, as if it were my own sentence I was to hear, as in a manner it was. "I am a great sinner," he sighed, "God only knows how great. His punishment crushes me here that I may enter into His mercy hereafter."

He grew gradually calmer and began:

"Since my childhood I have been hot-tempered and violent. I could never endure contradiction, and was always ready to give a blow. But I have seldom let the sun go down upon my wrath, and I have never borne hatred toward any man. As a half-grown boy I killed our good, kind watchdog in one of my fits of rage for some trifling offense, and I have never ceased to regret it. Later, as a student in Leipzig, I let myself be carried away sufficiently to wound seriously my adversary in one of our fencing bouts. A merciful fate alone saved me from becoming a murderer then. It is for these earlier sins that I am now being punished, but the punishment falls doubly hard, now that I am an old man, a priest, a servant of the Lord of Peace, and a father! Ah, that is the deepest wound!" He sprang up and wrung his hands in deep despair. I would have said something to comfort him, but I could find no words for such sorrow.

When he had controlled himself somewhat he sat down again and continued: "To you, once my friend and now my judge, I will confess this crime, which it seems beyond a doubt that I have committed, although I am not conscious of having done so." (I was startled at this, as I had expected a remorseful confession.) "Listen well to what I shall now tell you. That I struck the unfortunate man with the spade, that he fell down and then ran away, this is all that I know with full consciousness. . . . What followed then? Four witnesses have seen that I fetched the body and buried it in my garden—and now at last I am forced to believe that it must be true. These are my reasons for the belief. "Three or four times in my life I have walked in my sleep. The last time—it may have been nine or ten years ago—I was to have held a funeral service on the following day, over the body of a man who had died a sudden and terrible death. I could not find a suitable text, until suddenly there came to me the words of an old Greek philosopher, 'Call no man fortunate until his death.' It was in my mind that the same idea was expressed in different words in the Holy Scriptures. I sought and sought, but could not find it. At last I went to bed much fatigued, and slept soundly. Next morning, when I sat down at my desk, to my great astonishment I saw there a piece of paper, on which was written, 'Call no man happy until his end hath come' (Sirach xi. 34), and following it was a funeral sermon, short, but as good in construction as any I have ever written. And all this was in my own handwriting. It was quite out of the question that anyone could have entered the room during the night, as I had locked it myself, and it had not been opened until I entered next day. I knew what had happened, as I could remember one or two such occurrences in my life before.

"Therefore, dear friend, when the last witnesses gave their testimony to-day, I suddenly remembered my sleepwalking exploits, and I also remembered, what had slipped my mind before, that on the morning after the night the body was buried I had found my dressing gown in the hall outside of my bedroom. This had surprised me, as I always hung it over a chair near my bed. The unfortunate victim of my violence must have died in the woods from his wound, and in my dream consciousness I must have seen this and gone to fetch the body. It must be so. I know no other explanation. God have mercy on my sinful soul." He was silent again, covering his face with his hands and weeping bitterly.

I was struck dumb with astonishment and uncertainty. I had always suspected that the victim had died on the spot where he was buried, although I could not quite understand how the rector had managed to bury the body by day without being seen. But I thought that he might have covered it lightly with earth and twigs and finished his work at night. He was a man of sufficient strength of mind to have done this. When the latest witnesses were telling their story, I noted the possible contradiction, and hoped it might prove a loophole of escape. But, alas, it was all only too true, and the guilt of the rector proven beyond a doubt. It was not at all impossible for a man to do such things in his sleep. Just as it was quite possible that a man with a fractured skull could run some distance before he fell to die. The rector's story bore the stamp of truth, although the doubt WILL come that he desired thus to save a shred of honor for his name.

The prisoner walked up and down the room several times, then stopping before me he said gravely: "You have now heard my confession, here in my prison walls. It is your mouth that must speak my sentence. But what says your heart?"

I could scarcely utter the words, "My heart suffers beyond expression. I would willingly see it break if I could but save you from a shameful death." (I dared not mention to him my last hope of escape in flight.)

"That is impossible," he answered. "My life is forfeited. My death is just, and shall serve as a warning to others. But promise me that you will not desert my poor daughter. I had thought to lay her in your arms"—tears choked his voice—"but, alas, that fond hope is vanished. You cannot marry the daughter of a sentenced murderer. But promise me that you will watch over her as her second father." In deep sorrow and in tears I held his hand in mine. "Have you any news from my son?" he began again. "I hope it will be possible to keep him in ignorance of this terrible affair until—until it is all over. I could not bear to see him now. And now, dear friend, let us part, not to meet again except in the hall of justice. Grant me of your friendship one last service, let it end soon. I long for death. Go now, my kind, sympathetic judge. Send for me to-morrow to speak my sentence, and send to-day for my brother in God, the pastor in Aalso. He shall prepare me for death. God be with you."

He gave me his hand with his eyes averted. I staggered from the prison, hardly conscious of what I was doing. I would have ridden home without seeing his daughter had she not met me by the prison door. She must have seen the truth in my face, for she paled and caught at my arm. She gazed at me with her soul in her eyes, but could not speak. "Flee! Save your father in flight!" was all I could say.

I set spurs to my horse and rode home somehow.

To-morrow, then!

The sentence is spoken.

The accused was calmer than the judge. All those present, except his bitter enemy, were affected almost to tears. Some whispered that the punishment was too severe.

May God be a milder judge to me than I, poor sinner, am forced to be to my fellow men.

She has been here. She found me ill in bed. There is no escape possible. He will not flee. Everything was arranged and the jailer was ready to help. But he refuses, he longs for death. God be merciful to the poor girl. How will she survive the terrible day? I am ill in body and soul, I can neither aid nor comfort her. There is no word from the brother.

I feel that I am near death myself, as near perhaps as he is, whom I sent to his doom. Farewell, my own beloved bride. . . . What will she do? she is so strangely calm—the calm of wordless despair. Her brother has not yet come, and to-morrow—on the Ravenshill—!

Here the diary of Erik Sorensen stopped suddenly. What followed can be learned from the written and witnessed statements of the pastor of Aalso, the neighboring parish to Veilbye.

PART TWO

It was during the seventeenth year of my term of office that the terrible event happened in the neighborhood which filled all who heard of it with shock and horror, and brought shame and disgrace upon our holy calling. The venerable Soren Quist, Rector of Veilbye, killed his servant in a fit of rage and buried the body in his garden.

He was found guilty at the official trial, through the testimony of many witnesses, as well as through his own confession. He was condemned to death, and the sentence was carried out in the presence of several thousand people on the little hill known as Ravenshill, here in the field of Aalso.

The condemned man had asked that I might visit him in his prison. I must state that I have never given the holy sacrament to a better prepared or more truly repentant Christian. He was calm to the last, full of remorse for his great sin. On the field of death he spoke to the people in words of great wisdom and power, preaching to the text from the Lamentations of Jeremiah, chap. ii., verse 6: "He hath despised the priest in the indignation of his anger." He spoke of his violence and of its terrible results, and of his deep remorse. He exhorted his hearers to let his sin and his fate be an example to them, and a warning not to give way to anger. Then he commended his soul to the Lord, removed his upper garments, bound up his eyes with his own hand, then folded his hands in prayer. When I had spoken the words, "Brother, be of good cheer. This day shalt thou be with thy Saviour in Paradise," his head fell by the ax.

The one thing that made death bitter for him was the thought of his children. The son had been sent for from Copenhagen, but as we afterwards learned, he had been absent from the city, and therefore did not arrive until shortly after his father had paid the penalty for his crime.

I took the daughter into my home, where she was brought, half fainting, after they had led her father from the prison. She had been tending him lovingly all the days of his trial. What made even greater sorrow for the poor girl, and for the district judge who spoke the sentence, was that these two young people had solemnly plighted their troth but a few short weeks before, in the rectory of Veilbye. The son arrived just as the body of the executed criminal was brought into my house. It had been permitted to us to bury the body with Christian rites, if we could do it in secret. The young man threw himself over the lifeless body. Then, clasping his sister in his arms, the two wept together in silence for some while. At midnight we held a quiet service over the remains of the Rector of Veilbye, and the body was buried near the door of Aalso church. A simple stone, upon which I have carved a cross, still stands to remind the passer-by of the sin of a most unfortunate man.

The next morning his two children had disappeared. They have never been heard of since. God knows to what far-away corner of the world they have fled, to hide their shame and their sorrow. The district judge is very ill, and it is not believed that he will recover.

May God deal with us all after His wisdom and His mercy!

O Lord, inscrutable are thy ways!

In the thirty-eighth year of my service, and twenty-one years after my unfortunate brother in office, the Rector of Veilbye had been beheaded for the murder of his servant, it happened one day that a beggar came to my door. He was an elderly man, with gray hair, and walked with a crutch. He looked sad and needy. None of the servants were about, so I myself went into the kitchen and gave him a piece of bread. I asked him where he came from. He sighed and answered:

"From nowhere in particular."

Then I asked him his name. He sighed still deeper, looked about him as if in fear, and said, "They once called me Niels Bruus."

I was startled, and said, "God have mercy on us! That is a bad name. That is the name of a man who was killed many years back."

Whereat the man sighed still deeper and replied: "It would have been better for me had I died then. It has gone ill with me since I left the country."

At this the hair rose on my head, and I trembled in every limb. For it seemed to me that I could recognize him, and also it seemed to me that I saw Morten Bruus before me in the flesh, and yet I had laid the earth over him three years before. I stepped back and made the sign of the cross, for verily I thought it was a ghost I saw before me.

But the man sat down in the chimney corner and continued to speak. "Reverend father, they tell me my brother Morten is dead. I have been to Ingvorstrup, but the new owner chased me away. Is my old master, the Rector of Veilbye, still alive?" Then it was that the scales fell from my eyes and I saw into the very truth of this whole terrible affair. But the shock stunned me so that I could not speak. The man bit into his bread greedily and went on. "Yes, that was all Brother Morten's fault. Did the old rector have much trouble about it?"

"Niels! Niels!" I cried from out the horror of my soul, "you have a monstrous black sin upon your conscience! For your sake that unfortunate man fell by the ax of the executioner!"

The bread and the crutch fell from his hand, and he himself was near to falling into the fire. "May God forgive you, Morten!" he groaned. "God knows I didn't mean anything like that. May my sin be forgiven me! But surely you only mean to frighten me! I come from far away, and have heard nothing. No one but you, reverend father, has recognized me. I have told my name to no one. When I asked them in Veilbye if the rector was still there, they said that he was."

"That is the new rector," I replied. "Not he whom you and your sinful brother have slain."

He wrung his hands and cried aloud, and then I knew that he had been but a tool in the hands of that devil, Morten. Therefore I set to work to comfort him, and took him into my study that he might calm himself sufficiently to tell me the detail of this Satan's work.

This was the story as he tells it: His brother Morten—truly a son of Belial—cherished a deadly hatred toward pastor Soren Quist since the day the latter had refused him the hand of his daughter. As soon as he heard that the pastor's coachman had left him, he persuaded Niels to take the place.

"Watch your chance well," he had said, "we'll play the black coat a trick some day, and you will he no loser by it."

Niels, who was rough and defiant by nature, soon came to a quarrel with his master, and when he had received his first chastisement, he ran at once to Ingvorstrup to report it. "Let him strike you just once again," said Marten. "Then come to me, and we will pay him for it."

Then came the quarrel in the garden, and Niels ran off to Ingvorstrup. He met his brother in the woods and told him what had occurred.

"Did anyone see you on the way here?" asked Morten

Niels thought not. "Good," said Morten; "now we'll give him a fright that he will not forget for a week or so."

He led Niels carefully to the house, and kept him hidden there the rest of the day. When all the household else had gone to sleep the two brothers crept out, and went to a field where several days before they had buried the body of a man of about Niel's age, size, and general appearance. (He had hanged himself, some said because of ill-treatment from Morten, in whose service he was. Others said it was because of unhappy love.) They dug up the corpse, although Niels did not like the work, and protested. But Morten was the stronger, and Niels had to do as he was ordered. They carried the body back with them into the house.

Then Niels was ordered to take off all his clothes, piece by piece, even to his shirt, and dress the dead man in them. Even his leaden earring, which he had worn for many years, was put in the ear of the corpse. After this was done, Morten took a spade and gave the head of the corpse two crashing blows, one over the nose, the other on the temple. The body was hidden in a sack and kept in the house during the next day. At night the day following, they carried it out to the wood near Veilbye.

Several times Niels had asked of his brother what all this preparation boded. But Morten answered only, "That is my affair. Do as I tell you, and don't ask questions."

When they neared the edge of the wood by Veilbye, Morten said,

"Now fetch me one of the coats the pastor wears most. If you can, get the green dressing gown I have often seen him wear mornings."

"I don't dare," said Niels, "he keeps it in his bed chamber."

"Well, then, I'll dare it myself," said Morten. "And now, go your way, and never show yourself here again. Here is a bag with one hundred thalers. They will last you until you can take service somewhere in another country. Go where no one has ever seen you, and take another name. Never come back to Denmark again. Travel by night, and hide in the woods by day until you are well away from here. Here are provisions enough to last you for several days. And remember, never show yourself here again, as you value your life."

Niels obeyed, and has never seen his brother since that day. He had had much trouble, had been a soldier and lost his health in the war, and finally, after great trials and sufferings, had managed to get back to the land of his birth. This was the story as told me by the miserable man, and I could not doubt its truth.

It was now only too clear to me that my unfortunate brother in the Lord had fallen a victim to the hatred of his fiendish enemy, to the delusion of his judge and the witnesses, and to his own credulous imagination.

Oh, what is man that he shall dare to sit in judgment over his fellows! God alone is the Judge. He who gives life may alone give death!

I did not feel it my duty to give official information against this crushed and broken sinner, particularly as the district judge is still alive, and it would have been cruelty to let him know of his terrible error.

Instead, I gave what comfort my office permitted to the poor man, and recommended him not to reveal his name or tell his story to anyone in the district. On these conditions I would give him a home until I could arrange for a permanent refuge for him in my brother's house, a good distance from these parts.

The day following was a Sunday. When I returned from evening service at my branch parish, the beggar had disappeared. But by the evening of the next day the story was known throughout the neighborhood.

Goaded by the pangs of conscience, Niels had gone to Rosmer and made himself known to the judge as the true Niels Bruus. Upon the hearing of the terrible truth, the judge was taken with a stroke and died before the week was out. But on Tuesday morning they found Niels Bruus dead on the grave of the late rector Soren Quist of Veilbye, by the door of Aalso church.

WHO WAS STEEN BLICHER?

Steen Steensen Blicher (1782–1848) was a Danish crime writer active in the early part of the Victorian Era. He is considered a trail blazer in Danish literature and is credited with pioneering the novella in that country as well as being one of the first crime writers and one of the first authors to employ the device of the unreliable narrator (which would be used later by the Modernists, notably Joseph Conrad in *Nostromo, Heart of Darkness* and other works). He was the son of a parson who could trace his lineage back to Martin Luther.

Most of his writing is set in Jutland, the name given to the peninsula that juts out in Northern Europe toward the rest of Scandinavia, forming the mainland part of Denmark. It has the North Sea to its west, Skagerrak to its north, Kattegat and the Baltic Sea to its east, and the Danish–German border to its south.

His writing is somewhat gloomy but this is probably due to the nature of his stories. His debut work, The Diary of a Parish Clerk was about a tortured peasant struggling to stay alive in the face of a meaningless universe. His follow up, The Hosier and his Daughter, was about a mentally troubled young woman who is driven insane by unrequited love. It was filmed twice in Blicher's lifetime.

But today he is remembered for *The Rector of Veilbye*. The novella is based upon a real life murder case from 1626 in Vejlby, Denmark which Blicher was familiar with from Erik Pontoppidan's Danish Church History (1741) and partly through oral tradition. Blicher's disturbing story has been adapted for the screen three times by Danish filmmakers in 1922, 1931 and 1972.

The original case upon which the story is based is the type of story that would make even the most weather-hardened Dane shiver. The trial of Pastor Søren Jensen Quist of Vejlby took place at Aarhus in 1626. The trial centered around the unexplained disappearance in 1607 of a farm laborer named Jesper Hovgaard who was employed at Pastor Quist's rectory. Fifteen years later, in 1622, human remains were unearthed on the grounds of the rectory. The bones were believed to belong to Hovgaard and word soon spread that the Reverend Quist had slaughtered him and tried to conceal the crime. During the police investigation, two local men, who had past animosity toward Quist, testified that they witnessed the cleric murder Hovgaard while in a drunken rage. The Reverend professed his innocence but was found guilty and executed by decapitation on July 20, 1626. In 1934, Quist's son who had become the Pastor of Vejlby discovered that the witnesses had been bribed and the two men whose false testimony sent the Reverend to his death were executed for perjury in 1634.

In 2006, The Rector of Veilbye was selected for inclusion in the Cultural Canon of Denmark by the Danish Ministry of Culture. During the ceremony, an official declared that, "the style illuminates elegiac pain and discomfort in an eerily intense drama, and the story is difficult to shake off."

Renowned Scandinavian critic Søren Baggesen stated "Blicher is not just the first of Danish literature's great storytellers, he is one of the few tragic poets, Danish literature has ever had."

Printed in Great Britain
by Amazon